This is me, Sam.
And this is a book I made
all by myself.

This book is for my mum.

SIMON AND SCHUSTER

First published in Great Britain in 2009
by Simon and Schuster UK Ltd
1st Floor, 222 Gray's Inn Road, London, WC1X 8HB
A CBS Company

Text and illustrations copyright © 2009 Michael Broad

The right of Michael Broad to be identified as the author and
illustrator of this work has been asserted by him in accordance
with the Copyright, Designs and Patents Act, 1988
All rights reserved, including the right of reproduction
in whole or in part in any form
A CIP catalogue record for this book is available
from the British Library upon request
ISBN: 978 1 84738 145 3 (HB)
ISBN: 978 1 84738 146 0 (PB)
Printed in China
1 3 5 7 9 10 8 6 4 2

All the books I've seen
have this, so I cut one
out and stuck it in . . .

MY BRILLIANT BOOK

by
Michael Broad

BY ME,
SAM

and this

SIMON AND SCHUSTER
London   New York   Sydney

One day, when my sister
Holly was reading a book,
I said, "I'M BORED!"
at the top of my voice.
"Well read a book then,"
she said.

Holly's book is pink and has fairies in it and looks like the most boring book ever.

This is our cat Carrot. He's called Carrot because he's orange.

"But all my books are boring!" I said, pointing at the pile of boring books under my bed.

A boring baby book about a duck for someone younger than me.

A boring book with loads of words and no pictures for someone older than me.

This one's really good but I've already read it a squillion times.

Holly waved one at me.

"Look, this one's about a train!" she gasped, as if a book about a train was the most exciting thing in the world!

"But it's just about a train," I said. "Which is not very interesting. Not half as interesting as . . ."

CHOO! CHOO!

MONSTERS

VROOM! VROOM! VROOM!

BIG BOOK OF STORIES

DINOSAURS

"A flying train driven by a pirate with two eye-patches who can't see where he's going, and all the people on the train are going,

ARRRRRGGGGGGHH!

That would be a brilliant book. I'd definitely read that one."

"Then maybe you should make your own book," laughed Holly.

"Maybe I will!" I said.

So I got out all my pens and paints, and I made two lists.

STUFF I DO WANT IN MY BRILLIANT BOOK

1. Funny stuff
2. Scary stuff (but not TOO scary)
3. Big stuff
4. Small stuff
5. Messy stuff
6. Exciting stuff
7. Stuff that is brilliant
8. Captain Blacklegs can be in it too if he wants because he's very friendly. You'll meet him on the next page.

STUFF I DON'T WANT IN MY BRILLIANT BOOK

1. Cabbage
2. Sprouts
3. Turnips
4. Ducks
5. FAIRIES!
6. Boring stuff
7. Stuff that is not brilliant
8. The dog who lives next door can't be in it because he always barks when I go past the gate.

I even stuck a chewed-up pencil behind my ear because that's what people who make books do.

A sweet for later.

I looked around my room and tried to think of a brilliant story.

This is Captain Blacklegs. He lives under my desk.

Then I had an idea about a dinosaur . . .

Once upon a time there was a dinosaur as big as a house.
The dinosaur was as big as a house because he'd eaten a house.
The house still had people living in it and they were are all blue
because they'd eaten too many blueberries . . .

Once upon a time there was a world made of sweets and the hairy monsters who lived there were allowed to eat all that they wanted. But they got really big like balloons, floated off into the sky and kept on going until they ended up in outer space . . .

Then I had an idea
about outer space . . .

Once upon a time there were some aliens who lived on the moon and had lots of eyes and no noses (aliens can look like anything you want as no one really knows what they look like). The aliens all had seven legs and argued about shoes all the time . . .

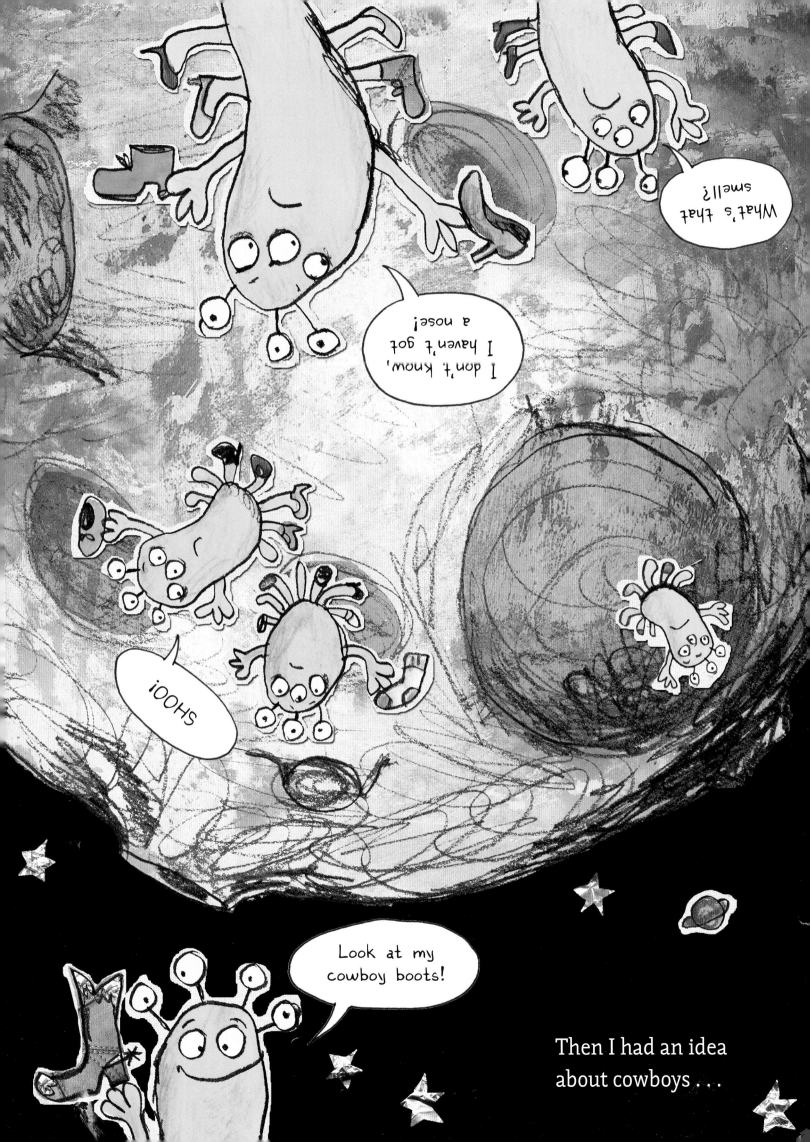

Once upon a time there were some cool cowboys living in the Wild West. The cowboys were so cool that, instead of horses, they rode giant bugs which they rounded up with magic lassoes . . .

To make the most BRILLIANT BOOK
EVER, I'd have to put ALL of these
things in it! EVERY SINGLE ONE!
So I made up a new story . . .

These are Carrot's
paw prints from
when he walked over
my desk.

There's a bit of space here
so I thought I'd show you
what Carrot looked like when
he came home from the vet
with a lampshade thing on his
head. He looked very cute.

Some mean aliens who lived on the moon were arguing about shoes and decided to invade the sweet world in their shoeships!

Luckily, some cool cowboys riding giant bugs turned up and lassoed the aliens. The monsters were so happy that they let the cowboys ride the house dinosaur.

I decided to show Holly my brilliant idea.
"Cowboys and aliens and bugs and monsters
AND a dinosaur who ate a house?" she frowned.
"You can't put ALL those things in one book."

"Why not?" I asked.
"Because a book has to make sense,"
she said. "And if it doesn't make
sense, people won't understand it."

Fairy Princess

When Holly wears her fairy
wings I call her BUG GIRL.
She gets VERY cross.

When I looked at it again, it seemed
Bug Girl was right. Making a book
with so much brilliant stuff in it
was impossible . . .

There wouldn't be
any blueberries or
even a cactus
in a world made
of sweets . . .

And a dinosaur
would much rather
eat a monster
than a house . . .

And the aliens
would ONLY want
to invade a world
made of shoes . . .

And the cool cowboys
belong in the Wild
West with their
giant bugs . . .

But...

then I realised something – I COULD
make a book with ALL that brilliant stuff
in it AND it would completely make sense!
All I had to do was . . .

BRILLIANT STUFF CHECKLIST!

- ☑ A CAT
- ☑ MR BRAINS
- ☑ A FLYING TRAIN
- ☑ A PIRATE
- ☑ A SPIDER
- ☑ A DINOSAUR
- ☑ BLUE PEOPLE
- ☑ HAIRY MONSTERS
- ☑ SWEETS
- ☑ ALIENS
- ☑ COWBOYS
- ☑ GIANT BUGS
- ☑ A TALKING CACTUS

Now think about all the brilliant stuff YOU like, and make YOUR BRILLIANT BOOK!